THE BLUE DRAGON

Library and Archives Canada Cataloguing in Publication

Tierney, Ronald, author
The blue dragon / Ronald Tierney.(Rapid reads)

Issued in print and electronic formats.
ISBN 978-1-4598-0904-8 (pbk.).—ISBN 978-1-4598-0905-5 (pdf).—
ISBN 978-1-4598-0906-2 (epub)

I. Title. II. Series: Rapid reads
PS3570.I3325B58 2015   813´.54   C2015-901560-X
C2015-901561-8

First published in the United States, 2015
Library of Congress Control Number: 2015934293

Summary: Forensic accountant Peter Strand investigates a suspicious
death in San Francisco's Chinatown in this work of crime fiction. (RL 4.3)

*Orca Book Publishers is dedicated to preserving the environment and has
printed this book on Forest Stewardship Council® certified paper.*

Orca Book Publishers gratefully acknowledges the support for
its publishing programs provided by the following agencies:
the Government of Canada through the Canada Book Fund and the
Canada Council for the Arts, and the Province of British Columbia
through the BC Arts Council and the Book Publishing Tax Credit.

Cover design by Jenn Playford
Cover photography by iStock.com

ORCA BOOK PUBLISHERS
www.orcabook.com

Printed and bound in Canada.

18 17 16 15 • 4 3 2 1

I went to the garden and looked out into the twinkling night. Something was changing. What I'd told Cheng Ye Zheng that afternoon in the bar...these were things I'd never told anyone. I'd told him about being four years old and standing outside the wrecked car and seeing my parents, remembering them not as humans but simply as masks. As pretend.

ONE

It wasn't my assignment, I was told, to find the murderer. The police were working on it. My job was to calm the tenants of the Blue Dragon apartment building—particularly a Mr. Emmerich.

My client, Mr. Lehr, owner of the small, oddly named piece of real estate, was a rich Caucasian who thought that because I was "Oriental," I would have more credibility with his mostly Asian tenants than he would.

He was likely wrong on that matter. My parents were Chinese, but they died before

I knew them in any meaningful way. I was raised by a wealthy white family in Phoenix and went to a school dominated by children of wealthy white parents in Scottsdale. Though I was now in San Francisco, a city one-third Asian, many of them "fresh off the boat," as some would say, I could not speak Chinese in any dialect. Another problem with the situation was that while I was an investigator, I did so in high-finance and accounting circles. I had no experience on the tough, sometimes murderous streets of San Francisco, let alone in Chinatown, an area of the city about which I knew little.

It was twilight. The neon signs were just beginning to glow above the brick streets. There was a trading company, displaying goods in a yellowed, smoke-coated window. There was a flower shop with its door open. There was activity inside the narrow space—big-leafed plants in big ceramic pots were being moved. Workers were chatting in a language that was, of course, Chinese, but as foreign to me as Swahili.

Another narrow street. Also quiet. This one was a bit more residential. Above me were apartment windows where I could see the bluish, quivering light of television sets. Voices. From other buildings came the sounds of mahjong, plastic cubes being rolled and gathered and rolled again amid a chorus of excited shouts.

I found my building. Four stories of plain brick facade painted a smoky blue. There were eight built-in mailboxes on one side of the recessed entry and eight buzzers on the other. In the middle was a huge iron gate, which protected a wood-framed glass door with numbers printed in gold leaf.

My client said I should buzz 1A. Mr. Leu, the manager, would help me with whatever I needed. A balding man about sixty answered the door.

Before I could say anything, he spoke. Sadly, for me it was all gibberish.

"You here about 3B?" he asked again, this time in choppy English.

"3B?"

"Rent?"

"Rent? No. I'm Peter Strand. Mr. Lehr sent me over to talk with your tenants, to calm them down."

"Oh. Not expect you so soon, Mr. Strand."

He spoke English like Chinese characters usually spoke in old American movies. At first I thought it was a joke. Was Mr. Leu mocking me? I was never able to settle that little debate in my mind.

He smiled.

"You expected a white man?" I asked.

He nodded, smiling. Then shrugged. He looked at me more closely. "Come in," he said, moving to the open door near the entry. It was his apartment.

"You want tea? Beer?"

"No. But thanks." The place was small, a studio, I guessed. My client said Ray Leu got the apartment free and received a small sum for watching over the property. My client had also given me some background on all the other tenants—how long each had lived there, what they paid in rent, the level of difficulty they presented to management.

"Call me Ray," the man said. A cheerful man, he was no taller than I, but he seemed larger. It was his head, perhaps, bigger than usual. He wore work clothes—a blue cotton shirt that matched his grubby blue trousers. As we shook hands, I could feel the calluses. It wasn't difficult to imagine him wrestling water heaters and steam pipes.

"Ray is my American name," he said. "So you call me Ray."

"All right." All I wanted was to get this over with. Have the interviews with the tenants.

Tell them the owner was concerned. And that everything was all right.

"You are a private detective." He smiled. "A Chinese detective. But you don't speak Chinese?"

"You can't be sure of that, can you?"

He laughed deeply. He was proud of himself.

"No accent. The way you walk. You look uncomfortable outside waiting at the door. Clothes..." He shook his head. "Armani?"

"Not this one," I said. "Maybe you should be the detective."

"I would be a good detective, Mr. Strand." He looked around his small room, but he was pretending to see outside the walls. "This is one crazy house, you know?"

"Not yet."

He laughed again, pounding his thigh. "Mr. Strand, private eye." He laughed at what was apparent foolishness to him.

It seemed good-natured nonetheless. I took no offense. "You want me to show you where I found the body?"

"Please." The idea that I was looking at the scene of a murder was absolutely new and still unfathomable. I was a white-collar investigator, employed by CEOs and venture capitalists. I worked for anyone who wanted to invest in other people's businesses and other people's ideas. I did background checks in a process known as due diligence. My card did not say *private investigator*. It said *consultant*.

Even so, I did know a little about the crime. Mr. Lehr told me that a blow to the head had killed Ted Zheng, a tenant. The apartment manager had found the young man's body in the cellar at 5:45 AM about two weeks ago.

The police investigated and determined that the death was gang related. Drugs had been found in Ted Zheng's system.

Police assumed he was a "player." If they were right, finding the murderer would not be easy for the police. For me, it would be impossible. Yet the tenants were concerned.

This was to be a short assignment— drop in a few times, ask some questions. From my client's point of view, it was public relations. As Ray and I went down the uneven stone steps into the darkness, the broad beam of his flashlight lit only the immediate space before us. I noticed his dusty boots and my comparatively dainty Italian loafers.

"These steps were here before the earthquake. All of Chinatown was on fire. Everything gone but these steps," Ray exaggerated as we descended. "Nothing but rubble."

"Why is there no light?"

"Electrician come to work. Spend two hours. Screw up, then say he will be back. That was a month ago."

"Was the electricity out when Ted was killed?"

"Yes. Big problem. Wait long time. Elevator. Apartment? Ted was supposed to paint. He died. Problems."

"Death is a pretty decent excuse," I said.

"Cannot rent 3B until we find someone to finish the painting."

"You don't do that?"

"Not part of deal. Boss say I am not a painter. Touch up, maybe."

We crossed a stone floor.

"You carry a gun?" he asked.

"No."

There was silence for a moment. And I suddenly felt uneasy. I was in an absolutely foreign place within a foreign place. We were in total darkness. He controlled the only light. And why was he asking whether I had a gun?

The circle of golden light preceded us in sudden jerks of illumination. When the light splashed over a form in the corner, it went out as suddenly as the body appeared.

I must have made a sound.

Ray laughed.

"I put that there to show everyone where body was."

He flashed on the light. The form was a pile of clothes, loosely formed to suggest a body. I was beginning not to like Ray.

"Don't do that, Ray," I said.

"Private eye. Dangerous job," he said, still laughing. "Tough guy."

"The way we came in…is there any other way in or out?"

"You know what we say in China?"

"Give me the flashlight," I said, ignoring his question. What I wanted to do was bounce it off the top of his large laughing head. Instead, I slowly examined the walls and floor. No windows. No other way out.

Not much to examine. That was a good thing. I had no idea what I was looking for.

In a far corner there were paint cans, a ladder, brushes and roller trays. There were old doors and a ladder stacked against one wall, some pieces of molding, a dusty commode and some plumbing pipe. There was a table. Nothing was on it. A beat-up chair was near but facing away from the table. The tabletop was dusty. The seat of the chair wasn't.

"Anyone clean up after the murder?"

"Police, medical examiner, some guy with camera. But they didn't take anything. Body only."

"No blood?" I kept the flashlight and started back up the stairway.

"No." He followed me quietly. When we were at the top of the stairs, he paused in the entryway. "Very sad. I don't like to think about it. I try to make it funny, you know?"

TWO

The sun had fallen by the time I left Ray and his practical jokes. Darkness prevailed in the dimly lit alley. The plastic clicking sound of mahjong tiles still spilled out of upstairs windows. I walked over to and then up Grant Street toward Broadway. I'd have a bite to eat at Enrico's.

While I had a glass of Cabernet and some pasta, I glanced at the list Ray had drawn up for me—tenants and their phone numbers. Ray and I had drafted a note he'd slide under their doors in the morning, a short note saying that I had been sent to investigate the death of Ted Zheng and that I would call them to set up a time to discuss the tragedy.

I glanced through the list before I left. Most were Chinese names, but simple enough that I wouldn't stumble on their pronunciation. It was then that I noticed the name Cheng Ye Zheng, listed for 2A, and remembered that the victim's parents lived in the building. The victim, Ted Zheng, had lived in 1B. So did his lover, a Sandy Ferris.

During the first few sips of wine and while I waited for my dinner, I unfolded Ray's list and looked at the names again.

I added Ray's name. It read like this:

1A—Ray Leu. Apartment manager.

1B—Sandy Ferris. Social worker. Ted's girlfriend.

2A—Mr. and Mrs. Cheng Ye Zheng. Store owners. Ted's parents.

2B—Norman Chinn. Professor. And Steven Broder. Caterer.

3A—David Wen. Investment counselor. And wife May Wen. Retail.

3B—Unoccupied.

4A—Barbara Siu. Unemployed. Linda Siu. Attorney. Sisters.

4B—Wallace Emmerich. Retired.

Wine usually gave me a pleasant buzz. This time it didn't. Ray's clown act, his tiny, windowless apartment and the bizarre practical joke didn't sit well with me. Maybe it was deeper. Maybe the idea that life was so disposable. Someone had bludgeoned all the life from Ted Zheng and left his carcass crumpled in a dark corner of a cellar like a broken commode.

I thought there were other factors at work as well. Things having to do with Chinatown. About being Chinese. I didn't want to go there.

The next morning I slept late. The heavy food. The wine. I dreamed, but whatever ephemeral reality I visited in my sleep was lost as I stepped into the light streaming through the kitchen window.

First things first. After my first sip of coffee I picked up the telephone. I found the number in the notebook. I dialed. A voice identified the homicide department.

"Inspector O'Farrell?"

"Speaking."

"I'm Peter Strand. My client, Mr. Lehr—"

"Yes. He said you'd call. About Ted Zheng?"

"Yes. I just want you to know that I'll be talking to some people about the death—I wanted to let you know before you heard it from someone else."

"Glad you called." There was a practiced civility in the gravelly voice. It wasn't exactly warm or friendly. "You know it's an open case, Mr. Strand. So if you decide to go wider than the apartment building, I would appreciate it if you check in with me."

"I will. You mind if I ask a couple of questions?" I wanted to be as knowledgeable as I could before interviewing the tenants.

"Fire away," O'Farrell said.

"It is my understanding that he was killed by a blow to the head?"

"Compound fracture, hematoma."

"Was the weapon found?"

"No."

"Do you have any theories about what kind of weapon it was?"

There was a long pause. No doubt the inspector was deliberating—how much should he tell?

"Actually could've been anything. Baseball bat. Pipe."

"Something hard and round?"

"Right."

"No witnesses."

"A couple of rats maybe."

"Mr. Lehr said you thought it was gang related?"

"He had drugs in his system. Meth. Drug deal gone south looks to be a good possibility."

"You don't think the drugs could have been recreational?"

"Aren't they all? Listen, we can't be sure. But Zheng was a player. Strictly minor league. Gambling, mostly. Wasn't a violent guy. No felonies. But he played around the edges, and he knew a lot of questionable types, if you know what I mean. Beyond that things get hazy. Pure speculation."

"Anyone closer to home?"

"Who? We checked out the girlfriend. Belongs on a Wheaties box. Family is decent, trying to make a living. They loved the kid. Nobody else would have a motive. He was a likable guy is what I hear. Charm.

Wasn't coming down on anybody who lived in the building as far as I could tell."

"Any leads?"

"No. If it's gang related, it might come out in the wash tomorrow or years from now. Who knows? We've asked around. If anybody saw anything, nobody's talking."

"So you don't mind me meddling a little bit?"

"You find something, let me know. And Mr. Strand, if you get a chance, try to get this character Wallace Emmerich off my butt."

I recognized the name. Emmerich had been complaining to Mr. Lehr as well. Emmerich, Lehr told me, had owned the building before he did. Lehr had told me a few other things as well. One of those things was that Emmerich just loved to complain.

THREE

After talking with the police, I retrieved the list Ray had made for me and began calling tenants. I started with the victim's parents.

The greeting was in Chinese.

I spoke English slowly. "Mrs. Zheng, my name is Peter Strand."

A flow of Chinese words. I couldn't be sure, of course, but there seemed to be anger or frustration in the tone.

"My name is Peter Strand," I said even more slowly and caught myself speaking louder. I knew better.

This time there was a short burst of Chinese, and then she hung up.

The next logical call went to the girl-friend, Sandy Ferris. An answering machine picked up. The message wasn't personal-ized. It was the factory-made voice asking me to leave a message. I did.

Next on the list was the prime trouble-maker, Wallace Emmerich.

He answered.

"My name is Peter Strand."

"Yes, yes. I found the piece of paper under my door," he said with obvious disgust.

"Mr. Lehr has asked me to look into the death of Ted Zheng."

"Three weeks after it happened."

"This is an active investigation. The police are still working on it, Mr. Emmerich."

"So they say."

"I wondered if I might set up a time to talk with you."

"I doubt if that would be of much help. I do not know anything about the life of young Mr. Zheng. I did not see or hear anything the night of the murder. So a visit would not prove productive for either one of us."

"It was my impression from the police and from Mr. Lehr that you are concerned about what happened."

"Concern about and knowledge of the event are two very different things."

"Perhaps you know more than you think you do, Mr. Emmerich, and I would—"

"I am aware of the extent of my knowledge—"

"Do you realize that everyone in the building is a suspect in the unfortunate death of Ted Zheng. And that includes you."

There was a moment of silence. Then laughter.

"I can see you today if you would like."

We set up a time.

I called all the others with minimal success. I left word on a number of answering machines. Calling during the day in the middle of the week was not necessarily a good idea. I caught a sleepy Steven Broder who wanted to call me back. His roommate, Norman Chinn, was at the university and would be back late afternoon.

I also talked to Barbara Siu, whose English was good enough to say that she would prefer I talk to her sister, who wouldn't be home until evening.

Wallace Emmerich was not what I expected. I'd imagined a large, robust pompous man. Instead, I found a small, frail pompous man. He sat in a large blue chair. He wore a black crushed-velvet jacket.

The door had been left ajar. Wallace Emmerich had answered my knock with a sharp command to enter.

"Mr. Emmerich, I'm Peter Strand."

"I know who you are."

"I have a few questions," I said.

The room was odd, memorabilia mixed with emptiness. There was a large photograph of Emmerich on a boat with an Asian woman. They were waving. There was another of Emmerich standing in an office with several men in suits. There were framed certificates of appreciation and commendation. There was a framed authentication of his degree in engineering. On one wall were floor-to-ceiling bookcases with books on commerce, international trade, shipping rates.

The dark, worn sofa and chairs were covered with leopard- and tiger-skin pillows. A heavy crystal-laden chandelier hung dustily but grandly from the center of the ceiling. There were large candelabra on the mantle and two marble lion dogs on either side of the fireplace. The fireplace contained ashes of probably a dozen fires.

Even so, the place seemed sparse. On the walls I could see rectangles of brighter wallpaper where paintings or mirrors had once hung. There was a glassed-in cabinet with nothing on its shelves. And a carpet remnant with ragged edges was in the hall that led to the bedroom and bath. It seemed completely out of place.

"You've expressed a great deal of concern to Mr. Lehr and the police about the death of Ted Zheng…"

"Yes, we've discussed that on the telephone, haven't we, Mr. Strand?"

"Yes. Are you aware of any difficulties Ted may have had with other tenants?"

"Ted had difficulties with all of the tenants at one time or another."

"I was under the impression that he was a likable young man."

"Oh yes," Emmerich said with some disdain, "he could charm the birds out of the trees."

"But not you?"

"I have associated with many and varied people in my life. I headed up Far Eastern Operations for a rather large multi-national corporation in Hong Kong. And later in Mainland China. I'm not easily flattered into acquiescence."

"What kind of things did Ted Zheng try to get you to go along with?"

"He'd simply try to sell me used items of one sort or another."

"What kind of items?"

"Antiques, Mr. Strand."

"He wanted you to buy antiques from him?"

"Yes. I didn't realize my comments had been ambiguous."

"Your wife?" I asked, nodding to a photograph of an Asian woman just behind him on a shelf.

"Yes." He didn't need to look. "We were married for twenty-five years." His brief smile turned quickly to a frown. "She died not quite ten years ago."

"I'm sorry."

"You knew her, did you?" he asked, fully aware that I did not.

"No. An expression."

"An empty one."

I wanted to say that she probably died to escape him, but I didn't. He continued on his own, more or less talking to himself.

"She was a little older than I. She looked younger," he said softly. Then, as if suddenly aware that I was in the room, he continued loudly, "But age was not kind to her mind."

"How long have you lived here?"

"Fifteen years," he said. "When I retired."

"You were young," I said.

"What do you mean?"

"I mean to have retired. You were very young. Still young," I added to avoid offending him.

"I'm sixty-five," he said.

Actually, he was much younger than I'd thought. I had guessed him to be in his mid to late seventies. He seemed older than my stepfather, who was in his eighties.

"You've seen a lot of people come and go here?" I suggested, trying to get him to talk more about the building and the people in it.

"Surprisingly, most of the people who come here stay here. The Siu sisters were here before me. And the Zhengs. Mr. Chinn has been here twenty years or so. His friend is more recent," Emmerich said with derision. "On the floor below, there is a young Chinese couple who have been here for five years. I've heard they want to move to Pacific Heights or something."

"That leaves the empty apartment and Sandy Ferris."

"Sandy, is it? Well, I didn't even know her name. She lived with Ted. He's had others. Hard to keep track. Ted got that apartment through his father."

"And the empty apartment?"

"That's been empty for months. I don't think they're trying especially hard to rent it. You might mention to your Mr. Lehr that he's let this building go to seed. The elevator is in disrepair."

"Who lived there?"

"The elevator?" Mr. Emmerich said, straight-faced and more than willing to point out my conversational leap in logic.

"If you wish," I said.

He overlooked my impudent reply and seemed quite content with showing his superior mind.

"For years it was the Ongs. A sweet older couple. She died. Then Mr. Ong nearly burned the place down. The children came to get him. Then Mrs. Ho lived there. She was quite old and quite ill. She died there."

"I understand you once owned the building."

"Yes. The building became merely a number of petty annoyances. So I sold it to Mr. Lehr. Unfortunately, he hasn't the sense of responsibility I'd hoped for. And Ray would rather spy on the tenants than take care of the maintenance. You can tell them both what I've said, if you like."

"Thank you very much for your time, Mr. Emmerich. I hope you don't mind if I get back in touch with you if I have more questions."

"It's quite all right, Mr. Strand. By the way, do you speak Mandarin or Cantonese?"

"Neither," I said. "I don't speak Chinese."

"Truly?" he asked. "I speak both."

On the main floor I ran into Ray. He came out of his apartment as I stood in the entry trying to figure out the layout of the building.

"Two apartments on each floor?" I asked Ray.

"Yes. On main floor they are studios. Mine and Ted's."

It figured. The first floor was set in a bit. There was the entry area, the elevator, which had a sign saying OUT OF ORDER, and the stairway. Again I noted how Ray's door faced the entry. If he looked through his little peephole, he could easily see who came and went—as he had no doubt seen me now.

The front door opened. A man came in carrying a briefcase. He seemed hurried.

"Mr. Chinn," Ray yelled out.

The greeting seemed to surprise Chinn. He stopped suddenly on the stair up to the second floor

"This is Peter Strand," Ray said in an uncharacteristically formal manner. "And this is Norman Chinn."

Chinn eyed me for a moment, then seemed to shake off whatever had preoccupied him.

"Nice to meet you, Mr. Strand. I received Ray's note."

"You're in a hurry?" I asked, hoping I could get more than one interview out of my trip to Chinatown.

"Well…I guess not in that much of a hurry. I mean, if we need to talk, then I guess we might as well."

He looked around. My guess was he was trying to find a place to hold the conversation without inviting me up to his apartment. In the end, it was obvious there was no convenient place.

"I'm on two," he said.

I followed him up the narrow stairway.

"I have a few minutes," he said as we reached the top. "That's probably all you'll need. I really know nothing about this whole affair."

The layout of Norman Chinn's apartment was identical to Wallace Emmerich's. Outside of the placement of the walls, though, nothing else was the same.

The space was airy. The colors in the room were various shades of muted citrus. Walls and furniture and art were tied together by various shades of orange and lime and lemon. The living room was uncluttered and immaculate.

"You have a very nice place," I said.

"Steven and I have put so much into it—we've tiled the bath, completely redone the kitchen—that we really can't afford to leave."

He dropped his briefcase at one end of the sofa. "Please have a seat," he said, heading toward another door. "May I get you something to drink? Scotch, juice, a cola, water?"

"No, thank you," I said.

He came back in with a small plastic bottle of water. He set it down briefly while he removed his suit coat and loosened his tie.

"I was very sorry about Ted," Chinn said.

"You knew him?"

"Yes, Steven and I had him paint the apartment just...mmmn...two months ago."

"He did good work," I said.

"All right, I think. Jack-of-all-trades."

"Ted didn't talk to you about anything that troubled him?"

"No. Ted never had any troubles—or so it would seem. Positive, optimistic, always on the go. Always had a deal going that promised to make him a million."

"A slightly criminal edge to his deal making maybe?" I suggested.

"I have the impression that he appreciated shortcuts. Ted didn't go into detail. But he wasn't the type to be tied down to a nine-to-five kind of job. He lived by his wits." For a moment, Chinn seemed lost in his thoughts. "Perhaps he died by his wits.

Murder." He shook his head. "Such a horrible thing for the Zhengs."

"And for Sandy Ferris."

"I'm sure," Chinn said distantly.

"You've lived here quite a while," I said.

"I've been here twenty years, and Steven for fourteen. I was ready to move out, get a bigger place. Steven wanted to stay. He wanted to live in Chinatown." Norman Chinn smiled. "What else can I tell you, Mr. Strand?"

"I'm trying to get an honest picture of Ted," I said. "The police believe he was involved in a drug deal and that he was involved in gang activity. That doesn't seem consistent with your assessment."

"No, it doesn't. But then...today, who knows?"

"You're a professor?"

"I teach linguistics and deal with the problems of language for immigrants."

"I ran into that very problem with Mrs. Zheng."

The professor nodded. "Yes, it is hard for older people to learn new languages. You speak excellent English. I'd say second- or third-generation Chinese."

"Second. But I didn't know my parents. And I'm afraid I don't know Chinese at all. When was the last time you saw Ted?" I wanted to change the subject.

"I don't know exactly," he said after a few moments. "Probably a day or two before it happened. In the hall somewhere or on the stairway."

"What would Ted be doing on the stairway?" I asked, knowing that the young man lived on the first floor.

"He got around, that boy," Chinn said. "Running errands for Emmerich. Seeing his son."

"What?"

"His son. His mother, Mrs. Zheng, takes care of the child most of the time."

"Sandy's child?"

"Oh no. Before Sandy. About four years old, I'd guess. An all-Asian child. No doubt about it."

I'm sure a seasoned homicide investigator would have asked much more. But I was out of questions. The fact that Ted had a child had stopped me short but hardly shed any new light on the death. I wouldn't be adding the four-year-old to the list of suspects.

FOUR

Ray was in the entry, pushing a dust mop over the dull gray-tile floor, when I reached ground level. I doubted Ray was normally so industrious. He was waiting for me. Waiting to give and receive information. Gossip.

"When was the last time you saw Ted Zheng?"

"You mean alive?"

"Yes."

"That evening. Maybe eleven or eleven thirty," Ray said.

"He was the last one to come home?"

"I didn't say he went out."

"He was last person you saw?"

"The last one." He nodded. "No more come in."

"You're sure about that?" I asked.

"Very sure."

"How can you know that for certain?"

"I know," he said. "I hear."

"You can't hear everything." It irritated me that he should be so sure about something he couldn't be sure about. "You could have been out on an errand or eating dinner or something."

"I am here. I don't go out."

"You could have been in the shower or watching television or on the phone and missed it."

Ray shook his head.

"You can't have your eye glued to the little hole in the door twenty-four hours a day."

Ray shook his head. "You tell no one," he said in a conspiratorial whisper. He nodded for me to follow him. He led me to the front door and the iron gate. He showed me the wire that ran from the gate, up the wall, around the ceiling and down the wall to the doorway of his apartment. I followed him inside his small room. There was a switch.

"If front door opens. Light and buzz. Every night," Ray said, "I turn this on at 8:00 PM. I know who comes and who goes."

"You watch everyone who comes and goes?"

Ray shrugs. "My job."

"What if they come in the back door?"

"Sets off a fire alarm. Much louder. Everyone hears."

"And the fire escape?"

"Same thing."

"You do this wiring yourself?"

"Yes. Easy."

"Anyone come in that night who didn't live here?"

"No one."

"Who came in late?"

"David Wen from 3A. Mr. Broder in 2B came in very late."

"Is that unusual for Mr. Broder?"

"No. Unusual for Mr. Wen. He come home maybe ten o'clock, maybe even eleven. I think maybe he come back from a trip. He carry suitcases."

Certainly I'd have to reassess a few things. One was Ray. Perhaps he was a good deal brighter than his clown act suggested. I also wondered what other kind of snooping he did.

One of my thoughts had been that the murderer was a late-night visitor whose connection to the victim was known only by the victim. That was the police theory as well. But Ted Zheng died sometime after 10:30 PM and before 6:00 AM the next morning, and no strangers had entered the apartment building, if Ray was to be believed. Also, by midnight everyone who was going to be home *was* home, and no one had left prior to the discovery of the body.

I asked to see the rooftop. The door to the roof was on the inside, and it *was* locked, Ray said, when the police arrived and did their investigation.

There was a relatively small rooftop garden. Ray told me Mr. Emmerich took care of it. That he grew his own vegetables despite the less-than-pricey abundance available at nearby stores. There was nothing unusual up there.

I put Ray outside the circle of suspects. If he was the killer, he would not have narrowed the suspects to those who lived in the building. It would be easier to suggest the police were right—that some thug from Ted's supposedly shadowy world was the culprit.

Thanks to Ray, I knew the name and location of Mr. Zheng's shop. It was only a few blocks away—on Grant. There was a handmade sign in English—YOUR NAME IN CHINESE—just inside the doorway. Otherwise there was little else that might please the average family from Cleveland. No fake jade dragons, no ceramic tortoises, no brass Buddhas, no cotton T-shirts or wooden back scratchers. This was a stationery store. And there were papers of various kinds and cards with various Chinese symbols printed on them.

There was a young woman and an older man. Determining which was Mr. Zheng was not difficult. He was a handsome man with silver hair. He wore black pants and a white starched shirt.

"I'm Peter Strand. Mr. Lehr has asked me to look into the death of your son. I'm terribly sorry about your loss," I blurted, running the words together quickly. I felt awkward. It was if the meaning of Ted's death had quite abruptly hit me. This was the victim's father. Who was it that said, *At least a shallow man knows his depths?*

Mr. Zheng nodded.

"If you are too busy, we could set up a time to talk." I was hoping he'd say he was too busy. And I would escape. And I would not drag this man or his family into my little hustle. And that's exactly what this was beginning to feel like. What had I done with my principles? I had little else. In my quiet little anal-retentive life, I had nothing but my work and my…honor.

Mr. Zheng looked around. He said something in Chinese to the young woman and came from behind the counter. He put his hand in the small of my back and guided me gently and warmly toward the door.

"We can go somewhere," he said, "where it is more comfortable. Have you eaten?"

It was nearly three o'clock, somewhere between lunch and dinner. I wasn't hungry, though I should have been. We went to the

Orient Cafe. It was like a movie set. Huge, heavy, dark chandeliers hung over the worn black-and-white-checked floor. The walls, a smoky rose, were in need of a couple of coats of paint.

We went down past the bar, where a few Caucasians in short-sleeved shirts and Bermuda shorts sat talking, maps out. There were two white women at one of the round tables we passed on our way to a row of small enclosed rooms. Mr. Zheng and I went into room 23.

A man in a white apron brought menus and plates with napkins on them. He and Mr. Zheng spoke briefly. There were probably two dozen rooms like this, affording diners the ultimate in privacy. What secrets had passed within these dark wooden enclosures? What whispers of love? What conspiracies were discussed? What sinister plans were set down?

"I called your number, and I think your wife answered. I don't speak Chinese, so we didn't get very far," I told him. "I may have upset her."

Mr. Zheng smiled and shook his head.

"She is very angry. Angry at Ted."

"Why?"

"Because he left her."

I thought I understood the oddness of his reply, but I didn't get it all.

"With the child?"

"That's what she says, but it is because he left. She believes he made certain choices, that in some way he chose to die. She is difficult. If it weren't for the child, she would have nothing."

Just then an older, very stern-looking Chinese man in a black suit and tie came in. He smelled of tobacco.

Mr. Zheng and the man talked. Soon the two of them were laughing.

I ordered some fried rice. Mr. Zheng, I came to understand when the order arrived, wanted only a beer.

"I can't drink at home," he said. "What would the child think?" He shook his head. "My wife, she is very difficult. She is old China. That was the problem, Mr. Strand. Ted was young America." Mr. Zheng was silent for a moment. "Entrepreneur," he said.

"You have any ideas about what may have happened?"

"No, I don't. One minute he was going to make a fortune with a nightclub. The next he was going to get a fleet of limousines. What a boy!" Mr. Zheng said that with a mix of exasperation and admiration. "Ted was so smart, so quick, so charming. But he bounced from one idea to another. From one person to another. No one could keep track of him."

"I hate to bring this up, but he police suggest that maybe he was dealing drugs."

"No," Mr. Zheng said clearly. "Nothing to hurt anyone else. Maybe himself. But he wouldn't get into drugs or prostitution. I know him. I knew him."

"Gambling?"

"Maybe. But nothing serious. A little mahjong maybe."

"And his girlfriend, Sandy?"

"What about her?"

"Do you and your wife like her, accept her?"

"My wife, no. Me? I accepted it as part of Ted's curiosity. He had a Chinese wife before. He wanted something different."

"Not serious?"

"Not serious, I'm sure."

"The people who live in the apartment building. Was Ted close to any of them, or did he have business with them?"

"All of them, one way or another. Ted was the kind of person who loved an audience. And people liked him. He was a charmer."

Mr. Zheng slipped into his own world but was brought out of it again when the waiter reappeared with another bottle of beer. The two talked more. My guess was that Mr. Zheng frequently came here for a few illicit beers.

"Come with me," Mr. Zheng said after we'd finished. "We'll talk with Gong Li. My wife."

We walked over to Stockton Street. Here the fruit and vegetables spilled from the markets out onto the narrow sidewalks, which were already too narrow to convey the massive river of people without creating bottlenecks.

There is in Chinatown, like in other neighborhoods, a recognizable, telltale scent. I think perhaps it is some strange mixture of the sweet cookie dough and the open fish markets.

My upbringing in Phoenix hadn't prepared me for the live fish sold from barrels and buckets. My upbringing in waspish, cellophane-wrapped America had done little to prepare me for this vaster marketplace. There were kicking frogs under netting, turtles waddling over each other in shallow water and eels in deeper tin pans.

As we approached the door of the apartment building and Mr. Zheng fiddled with keys, I noticed the doormat for the first time. BLUE DRAGON, it said, the letters nearly obliterated by countless entrances and departures.

"Blue Dragon?" I asked.

"Oh, that. Yes, that has been here for a long time. I don't remember now who did it. I guess someone just decided to name the building Blue Dragon. We are now entering the mouth, I suppose," he said with a laugh.

Ray was nowhere to be seen. I wondered if he was peeping from behind his door.

We went up the steps to the second floor.

"You know the other tenants very well?"

"Not very well. We say hello and that's about all," Mr. Zheng said, fishing a breath mint out of his pocket. He gave me a smile that insinuated we were partners in crime.

The Zhengs' apartment was immaculate. Mrs. Zheng was standing when we came in. She was a small woman with fierce eyes. In tow was the child, in blue shorts and a starched white shirt. He looked up curiously. On the sofa was an elderly man. He smoked a cigarette, holding it in long bony fingers that were yellowed from nicotine.

There was the obvious introduction. I smiled and nodded. Mrs. Zheng remained standing, brittle against the outsider.

I dropped down on my haunches and extended a hand to the child.

"Hello, I'm glad to meet you. What is your name?"

The child continued to stare, an undecipherable look on his fresh face.

It seemed odd. I was his age when I last saw my parents. Now his too are gone, I thought. That was an assumption. I hadn't asked about the boy's mother, Ted Zheng's wife. That should have been too obvious to miss.

FIVE

It was an awkward visit. So much of the conversation had to be translated. Each of my questions caused considerable discussion before Mrs. Zheng would consent to answer.

A few important pieces of information emerged. Ted's wife had died in childbirth. Mrs. Zheng disliked Sandy Ferris and didn't want her to be with the child. Mrs. Zheng had seen her son earlier the day he died—in the afternoon.

The angry woman had nothing to say about any of the other tenants. But she turned up her nose when the Wens in apartment 3A were mentioned. There was much Mr. Zheng did not translate for me. During the long and animated conversations they had with each other, I glanced at the child. What would he remember of his father?

We were similar, this child and I. But he was being raised in a Chinese home. He knew his grandparents. He spoke the language. And perhaps, unlike me, his face would never be strange to him.

A photograph of Ted sat on a table nearby. He was in his late teens or early twenties, I guessed. He was handsome and smiling and with a woman I presumed to be the child's mother. The child. I thought of him as only "the child." I hadn't gotten his name—only his long and now curious look.

Coming out of the Zhengs' apartment I spotted what had to be Steven Broder,

fiddling with his key at the door of apartment 2B. He was wearing black pants and
a white shirt and tennis shoes. In his hand
were a black jacket and a pair of black shoes.

"Mr. Broder."

His head twisted around, and he looked
at me curiously.

"I'm Peter Strand."

He still looked puzzled.

"Investigating…"

"Oh yes," he said, relieved.

"Do you have a second to talk about
Ted Zheng's death?"

"A second, maybe a second and a half."
He paused in front of the door. It was
obvious we were going to have our conversation in the hall. "I don't have much to say."

"You knew him?"

"Yes, of course—he lived in the building."

"You knew him a little better than that,"
I said.

"What do you mean?"

"I mean, it was a little more than a hello in passing, wasn't it?" I had detected a defensive attitude, and I instinctively probed in the same direction that had gotten me that reaction.

"What are you getting at?" he said. "Listen, I'm doing a double today. I don't have much time, and frankly, I wasn't born with a lot of patience."

He started to turn to put his key in the lock. It was difficult, having to juggle his belongings.

"What I mean is that you hired him to paint the apartment, right?"

"I didn't. Norman did."

"Did you like Ted?"

"I didn't think much about him one way or another."

"Did you see him that night? The night of his death?"

"No," Broder said with quick certainty.

"You're sure?"

"What is this? I really know nothing about his death. I don't know much about his life. Now, I'm sorry if that seems callous, but unfortunately, life goes on, and so do I."

"I'm sorry about the inconvenience. Sometimes people see things they don't know they see and—"

"I'm sure that all makes for a very nice philosophical discussion, but I don't have the time. Talk with Norman." He'd finally gotten his key into the lock and was about to disappear.

"I have," I said.

He paused for a moment. He looked at me as if for the first time, up and down, appraisingly. "That's just fine and dandy."

"Weren't you a little closer to Ted?" I asked, probing without grounds.

"Not me, sweetheart."

Steven Broder was gone.

I waited at the door. In a moment I heard loud voices inside.

The Sandy Ferris who opened the door to apartment 1B on Saturday morning was a woman with bright-red hair and freckles. She had clear, bright-blue eyes and a smile. She wore a white T-shirt through which her obviously unencumbered breasts were visible. Below, an expanse of flesh, including her navel, revealed itself before disappearing into the loose waistband of a pair of tan shorts.

I suppose I expected an aura of grief wrapped in sackcloth. I didn't get that, nor did I get the image Norman Chinn had painted, of an all-American girl, the type you'd find on a Wheaties box.

"Come in," she said, and as I did, a gray cat with yellow eyes leaped to the back of the sofa, wary eyes focused on the stranger. The inside of the apartment was stark. Yet it had the requisite furniture—a sofa, side table with lamp, an upholstered chair. All from the same unidentifiable time period.

The large photograph stood out as ornament. It showed two barely clad individuals. One was Sandy Ferris, whose slender body seemed nevertheless to explode out of a skimpy bikini. The other was a muscular and handsome Ted Zheng. He too seemed to be attired in the minimal amount of fabric necessary to avoid arrest.

"Mexico," she said. "Acapulco."

I nodded.

"I'm sorry about Ted," I said.

She shrugged.

I interpreted it to mean "what can I say?" rather than that it was of no consequence to her.

"Sit down," she said, nodding toward the sofa. The cat came across the back of it and down the arm to greet me. Its nose touched my fingertip. Then it rubbed its face across my hand. It leaned its soft body into my palm as I ran it along its back.

I wasn't aware that I had thought so much about what kind of person Sandy Ferris would be. This was a social worker? This was a woman who had just lost her lover? Whatever I'd had in mind to ask her had vanished at the sight of the real person. It wasn't just the apparent sexuality and strange attractiveness that unnerved me. It was…yes, I expected sackcloth. I expected mourning. I did not expect sunlight and a sensuous woman.

The gray cat found its way into my lap.

"How long have you lived here?" I asked.

"Less than a year," she said, still standing. "Can I get you something? Coffee?"

"Thank you." That might give me a moment to get my mind together.

"He's lived here for a few years," she said from the kitchen. "I think it was late last fall that I moved in."

"So the photograph is recent?"

"Yes. February. We scraped some money together and went to Mexico."

"Where did you meet?"

"Where I work." She came in with two cups. "This is about an hour old," she said, sincere apology in her voice. "He wanted to get some help—day care or something—for his child."

"What about Mrs. Zheng?"

"Oh, she loves the boy—don't get me wrong." Sandy settled into the sofa at the other end. "But it's all so Chinese. Ted wanted his son to have a chance in America. Learn English before he went to school. He wanted Mark to be an American. Football, hamburgers, big-screen TVs. Mrs. Zheng isn't likely to let that happen. Ted really struggled when he was young."

"Struggled?"

"He said he always felt caught between the cultures. He wasn't educated the way he felt he should have been to succeed. He said he could have been a great businessman. But no one took him seriously. He used to say that he spoke English like a peasant."

"The police seem to believe that he was dealing drugs."

Sandy frowned. "No. Ted played with them. Parties. We'd go out. He'd do something to get in the mood, to stay in touch with the others."

"Didn't that mean he was hanging out with some pretty shady characters?"

"All middle-class partygoers," she said. "Like me. Not gangsters, not murderers. What we did was small. Really small."

"You party a lot?"

She smiled. "Weekends. Life's short. I work hard during the week. At night I try to forget all my troubles..."

"And try to get happy."

"Yes," she said, smiling, tilting her head and seeming to invite me to continue in that direction.

The cat rolled over on its back. I patted its belly. It wanted more.

"Ted's family. How do they feel about you?"

"The father is nice, polite. His mother hates me." She shrugged. It was her line now: "What can I say?"

"How did Ted get along with others in the building?"

"Pretty good. He did work for some of them from time to time."

"Who? What kind of work?" My ignorance was only partially feigned.

"He would find buyers for some of Mr. Emmerich's seemingly endless supply of antiques. He'd do some odd jobs for Ray. And painting for Steve and Norman."

"Anyone else?"

He helped Miss Siu's sister move in. And he helped Miss Siu get her pamphlets out. She's going to run for city supervisor."

"What about the Wens? Nobody seems to mention them."

"I don't know much about them," Sandy said. This reply was different. The tone wasn't casual, though Sandy tried to make it sound that way. It was hard for her to keep her teeth from clenching.

"Did Ted know them?"

"I don't know," she said coldly.

"When was the last time you saw Ted that night?"

"About midnight. He said he was going out for a while."

"He did?"

"Yes."

"At midnight?"

"Before, I think."

"Unusual?"

"No."

"Did he say where he was going?"

"No."

"Who he was going to meet?"

"He didn't say he was going to meet anyone."

"Did he often do that?"

She was no longer the open, friendly, flirtatious young girl. Sandy Ferris was uncomfortable.

"I told the police everything."

She seemed like a little girl. Now very unsure of herself. She had pulled her legs in, her body in full retreat.

"Did you tell them you had a fight?"

She waited. "Yes...sort of. It wasn't serious. He said he was going out for some fresh air. I didn't like him to smoke inside. Sometimes he'd only be gone for ten or fifteen minutes. This time it was longer."

"And it was before midnight?"

"Eleven thirty."

"You know that exactly?"

"Yes. I remember looking at the clock."

"Why did you look at the clock?"

"I don't know. Why do people look at the clock?"

"Maybe sometimes they look at a clock because someone else did. Ted looked at the clock, didn't he?"

I was prepared for either answer. But one would be more telling than the other.

"Yes," she said.

"And you didn't worry when he didn't come back?"

"Well…"

"Because he'd stayed away before?"

"Yes."

"And did you tell the police that?"

"Yes."

Seemed logical that the police, already determined to put him in their drug-dealer scenario, would take his strange comings and goings as support for their theory.

But if he'd left, actually left the building, Ray would have known it.

"Were you aware of any problems he might have had with the other tenants?"

Her hand went to the sleeping cat, still on my lap. Her palm swept back the smooth gray fur. I wasn't sure of her intent. It seemed intimate. I was growing uncomfortable.

"No," she said softly.

"Are you going to stay here?"

"I don't know," she said wistfully. "I don't know if it matters where I live."

She said it plainly, not with self-pity.

"Thanks for giving me the time. I'm really sorry to put you through—"

"You don't need to go."

"I need to go," I said. I really did. "I might need to talk to you again," I said.

"Please. Anytime. I'm up late."

I extricated myself from the sleeping feline.

I used the stairway to go from the first to the third floor, wanting to get a better sense of the building itself. It was a dark and dreary stairway.

I passed apartment 3B, the empty one. I was too early for the Wens, so I decided to check it out. The door opened without effort. Inside, the sun illuminated what appeared to be a relatively new paint job.

It had the same layout as Norman Chinn's. It was starkly white. On the floor was a drop cloth. I kicked the canvas, which also had newish spots of lime and lemon as well as dozens of other trampled-upon colors. In the folds of the cloth I noticed a piece of thin yellow cardboard. Just a torn edge. It was from a box. I recognized the color and a portion of the name Kodak.

I put it into my pocket as I looked around for signs of a struggle or blood. If there had been a struggle, there was nothing in the apartment to reveal it. There was no blood. I checked the bathroom. There were ashes in the sink. There was a cigarette butt floating in the toilet bowl. I poked it with a hanger. Filtered, but otherwise unidentifiable.

Of course it seemed strange that the first person I'd see after noticing this was someone with a cigarette.

SIX

May Wen was attractive. I guessed her to be in her late twenties or early thirties. But even if I were good at telling ages, it would be next to impossible to tell what lay beneath the heavy application of makeup. It was around noon on Saturday, and it looked to me as if she could be on her way out to a midnight soiree.

She puffed on a cigarette as we stood waiting in the living room for David Wen, her husband, to emerge from the bedroom.

"I don't have a lot of time," she said. "My boss is throwing a little brunch."

"It won't take long," I said. "How well did you know Ted Zheng?"

"One couldn't not know him," May said. "He's always around, always in your face."

"Did you like him?"

"I didn't dislike him," she said. "But we didn't socialize, if that's what you mean."

Her deep-colored lipstick matched her deep-colored fingernails. Her tight-fitting slacks were made of something shiny. Patent leather maybe. Latex. She spoke English like a native. No trace of an accent. I thought she might have come from Hong Kong, but what did I know?

"Did he ever work for you? Do odd jobs maybe?"

"No," she said vaguely.

"Painting? I understand he sometimes did that around the building."

"No, I do all the painting," David Wen said, coming into the living room carrying a Moschino suit bag and matching suitcase.

He extended his hand. David couldn't have been more different from May. He was dressed casually. He wore jeans, loafers without socks and a baggy sweater. Nice smile. Poised.

"We didn't know Ted very well," David continued. "We saw him in the hallways. Seemed okay."

"He was okay," May said. Her smile was to an imaginary audience, one her husband didn't see.

"I think he had a crush on May," David said. His tone was indulgent, amused, not jealous.

Her smile was hateful.

"I'm sorry. I shouldn't have said that. He seemed like a nice guy. I'm sorry about his death. Gruesome. Right here in the building." He shook his head.

"Did either of you see him on the night he died?"

"No," May said.

"No," David said. "I was out of town. I remember coming home the next day and May telling me about it."

"You travel in your job?"

"Some," he said.

"Some?" she repeated, rolling her eyes. "You practically live at the Ritz-Carlton."

"I'm not gone all that often. It's just that when I am, it's for long periods of time."

"How well did he get along with the others in the building?"

"I'm afraid I don't know much about the others in the building," May said. "Actually, this isn't my ideal place to live." She shot her husband a glance.

"We're looking." This was a response to May, despite his looking at me when he said it.

"Did the nature of Ted's death bother you much?"

"No. These things can happen anywhere."

I got the sense that this was an attractive couple riding high on the trends, living in the now of their choice. They wanted desperately to be or at least appear successful. This too made them seem an unlikely couple for Chinatown. Here, it seemed an older Chinese culture was struggling to hold on to its own way of life. These two didn't look like they wanted the old ways.

Now I was well ahead of my schedule. Too much ahead to intrude on the Siu sisters.

I went out for a walk. I had about an hour to kill. While I walked through the narrow and crowded streets, gathering in the smells, the faces, the foreign signs, I fingered the torn edge of the Kodak box in my jacket pocket. A connection with Ted. He'd been the one painting the apartment. When I returned to the Blue Dragon, Ray was waiting.

"What have you learned?" he asked, smiling. He was glad to have a co-conspirator. I was feeling a little smarmy with the association. But then, what was I doing? What business did I have digging into these private lives? And wasn't I beginning to enjoy it?

"Nothing much, but I have a question."

That made him happy.

"Ask me."

"Do the tenants socialize with each other?"

Ray looked puzzled.

"I mean, do the Siu sisters have dinner with the Zhengs, for example?"

A broad grin. "Noooooo," he said, shaking his head, laughing. When the laughter stopped, he looked particularly serious. "Very strange, these people. Very different from each other. I see them come in. Sometimes I see them on the stairs. They don't talk."

"It's unusual to have Caucasians in apartments here in Chinatown?"

His lips formed a frown that was intended to convey the seriousness of his thought.

"Quite true," he said, as if he were someone else suddenly. He grinned. "Miss Ferris. Mr. Broder. And Mr. Emmerich. Mr. Emmerich very different. He own this building once upon a time. Not so odd for him to live here. He live in China and he tell me one day he likes Chinese better than his own." Ray looked around the tiny lobby. "Strange, special place."

"Ted knew everyone though? Everyone?"

"Oh yes," Ray said. "Ted know everybody everywhere."

For all appearances, the Siu sisters lived in a copy shop. Stacks of brightly colored sheets of paper occupied nearly all the flat surfaces in the living room. LINDA SIU FOR SUPERVISOR, read the top sheet on one of the stacks. There were various proposition numbers on them. Most of the other stacks were obviously intended for a Chinese audience.

"Thank you for seeing me," I said to the two of them. They were polar opposites. One shrunk back, frightened. The other grabbed my hand the way a plumber or football player—or a politician, I guess— might. Firmly.

The shrinking violet was Barbara Siu. The glad-hander was Linda. She was the one running for a city supervisor slot, an important and prized office in San Francisco political circles. Dianne Feinstein launched her career from that board. She became mayor, then a powerful United States senator.

Certainly Linda Siu seemed serious about making a run. As I was to find out, she was a serious person in all respects.

There was no obvious place to sit down. For a moment I thought we'd have whatever conversation I was permitted while we stood there in the narrow pathway carved from the overwhelming abundance of political propaganda.

They led me, however, into the kitchen, where we sat around a small red Formica-topped table. The kitchen, smelling of ginger, pepper and other spices that I could not recognize, was a propaganda-free zone. It too was cluttered, but with things normally found in kitchens—or fairly normal.

As we sat, Linda asked, "You are aware that this is an active police investigation? Your involvement could be counterproductive, not to mention foolish."

"I've talked with the police. They've given me guidelines," I told her. "Other than interfering with their gang investigations, I have their blessing."

The demure sister readied some tea. Linda sat stiffly, hands folded on the table like a teacher waiting for the class to stop fidgeting.

"Then we might as well begin. What is it that you'd like to know?" she asked.

"I'd like to know how well you and your sister knew Ted Zheng."

"Fairly well. As well as you might know a neighbor, but not a friend," she said brusquely. "Ted helped me from time to time."

"Helped?"

"I say help, but what I mean is, he was paid to provide services—handling some of the copying arrangements, making some deliveries." She shook her head, more in frustration, it seemed, than sadness. "He was organizing a group of people to distribute flyers and buttons and hang banners. I don't know what I'll do now."

She shook her head again, this time to dismiss the thoughts. She seemed aware that she had veered away from the moment and was revealing an inherent coldness. Her concern was for her loss, not his or his family's.

"And your sister?" I asked as Barbara came to the table with the teacups and saucers.

There was some family resemblance. Barbara's face, for lack of a better way to describe it, was trapezoidal. She reminded me a bit of a fish underwater—hesitantly coming forward, then darting back. Linda's face was flatter. Yet I wouldn't doubt they were sisters for one moment.

"My sister," Linda said, "had little to do with Ted. He was kind of a blustery kind of fellow. Full of energy. Loud sometimes. I think my sister was frightened of him."

"Did she have reason?" I looked at the quiet sister, but Linda answered.

"No, not at all."

"What do you have to say, Barbara?"

Linda spoke again, this time to her sister, and in Chinese. Barbara spoke in return, now pouring pale green tea from the white teapot.

"She says he was a nice young man," Linda said, smiling. "She is sorry to hear that he has died. She said he brought her flowers once." Linda seemed surprised. "I didn't know that."

"When was the last time she saw him?"

More Chinese.

"She saw him that day. He came here to deliver some more pamphlets."

"Did he seem upset or worried or anything?"

I waited for the translation.

"No, he seemed normal."

"What about you?" I asked Linda.

"I'm not sure I saw him at all that day. I come and go. I work hard. Sometimes I don't know what day it is. But under no circumstances did I see anything I thought suspicious."

"He seemed very likable. I think everyone in the building liked him," I said, seeing if I could get any response.

"Well," she said, thinking as she spoke, "he was a likable sort. Young, immature—but his heart was in a good place, I suppose."

"Who were his friends in the building? You know, who did he hang out with?"

"I'm afraid I don't know."

"There was some indication that he used drugs," I said.

"Most people do, of one sort or another. I never saw him out of control."

"Are you a photographer by chance?"

She looked puzzled. Shook her head.

"I was thinking someone told me there was someone in the building who was an avid photographer."

"There might be. I don't know the other residents all that well."

"No one seems to know each other, but they all seem to have known Ted Zheng."

She was silent. It wasn't a question. And she wasn't going to answer it.

"I would think a politician like you would get to know everybody."

"Is that what you think?" she said curtly. "Thinking doesn't make it so, Mr. Strand."

A phrase my third-grade teacher had used.

"You have no thoughts about Ted Zheng's death?" I pressed.

"As I said, thinking doesn't make it true."

"Yes, but it might help us start down the path as we seek the truth," I said, hoping the sarcasm would bridge any gap in cultures.

"I'm afraid we can't help you."

"How's your campaign going?"

"Quite well, thank you," she said.

It was clear my time was up. That was fine by me. I couldn't think of anything else to ask.

"Thank you," I said, standing, my tea just now cool enough to drink. "I won't take up any more of your time."

"How soon will you be wrapping up your investigation?"

"Oh, I've just started," I said. "Unlike the police, I think the solution to this matter lies inside this building."

She blinked. For a split second, I saw surprise. For just that moment, I had a peek through the mask.

When I left, I passed by Mr. Emmerich's door. It was ajar as usual. I noticed that he was moving about. I crept a little closer to the door and looked in. He was moving an urn to the window. It couldn't have been an easy task. It contained a large fern and, I suspected, a decent amount of soil to sustain it.

SEVEN

I was most curious about the empty apartment. I hadn't thought to ask. And, too, my most ready access to information would come from Ray, ever eager to exchange gossip.

Ray found his way to me before I found my way to him.

"You find what you are looking for?" he asked. His face looked like those drawings of a happy sun.

"Bits and pieces," I said. "What about 3B? Who lived there?"

"Old Chinese woman."

"She moved?"

"She die."

"Here?"

He grinned again. "Accident. Fall down elevator shaft."

"And everyone believes it was an accident?" I wondered why Mr. Lehr hadn't told me about this. A death preceding a death, no matter how unrelated it might seem, ought to have been on his mind. Perhaps it was.

"Oh, Mr. Detective, honorable Mr. Chan, this is an old building. Elevator door work, elevator do not. Boom!" Ray clapped his hands together once.

"I think *splat* was the word you were searching for," I said, impatient with and unappreciative of Ray's gallows humor.

"That is why there is a sign on the elevator," he said, suggesting I had been more than remiss not to have figured it all out earlier.

"Thanks. When did she die?"

"About a month or so ago?"

"Ted Zheng was still alive then?"

"Yes. You think he did it?"

"That's not why I was asking. Did he know her?"

"Sure, he ran errands for her."

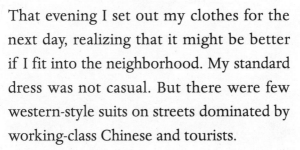

That evening I set out my clothes for the next day, realizing that it might be better if I fit into the neighborhood. My standard dress was not casual. But there were few western-style suits on streets dominated by working-class Chinese and tourists.

I also called my client, Mr. Lehr, and asked him why he hadn't bothered to tell me about the woman who fell down the elevator shaft.

"Not related," he said.

I didn't tell him that maybe that was why his tenants—actually, only Mr. Emmerich, as far as I could tell—were so upset. An elderly tenant lands at the bottom of an elevator shaft, and another is bludgeoned to death.

I wanted to know more about the so-called accidental death. And I was pretty sure I could find out.

When I pressed, Mr. Lehr told me more. The dead woman was Mrs. Ho. She'd been seventy-two and was becoming increasingly senile.

"She acted crazy," Mr. Lehr said. "I got calls from everybody about her. She was a problem."

"The problem was solved when she fell." Perhaps I was becoming too invested in this case. After all, I wasn't expected to solve crimes.

"There was a barricade in front of the door," Mr. Lehr fired back. "Not a big one, but big enough that no one but an idiot—"

"Or someone suffering from severe mental illness."

"—could miss it. Listen, safety inspectors and the police investigated. The elevator car was on four. The elevator technicians were working underneath and using the third-floor doors to move in and out. They took a break or something. She was just crazy. She belonged in a home."

"Wasn't anyone watching after her?"

"Toward the end, one of the Siu sisters helped her—helped with the groceries, paying the bills, that sort of thing. That kid, the dead kid, helped her."

That evening I kept a vigil outside the Blue Dragon. At ten thirty Norman Chinn came out. He was dressed casually. He walked down to California Street and hailed a taxi. Fortunately, it wasn't raining, and there were other cabs hanging around the gates to Chinatown. I calmly asked the driver to follow the other cab. I expected some kind of comment but got only silence until we arrived at a bar on Polk Street. Norman went inside. I counted to ten slowly before going in.

Not a woman in sight. On the dance floor was a mix of Asian and Caucasian men. Norman Chinn got a drink and went to the back of the bar, where a scantily clad young Asian boy danced for tips. I'd lived long enough in San Francisco to know there wasn't anything shocking about all this—but it was telling.

EIGHT

When I came back the next morning to stake out the apartment building, Sandy Ferris was bringing boxes out to the street. I stayed back. She was far too rushed and flustered to notice. In and out. The last few trips, she bore suitcases.

Seemed to me that if she had her entire life with her, it was a small life, materially speaking. She hadn't been too lucky in love either. In a few minutes she was done. She sat on the stack of boxes, looking tired, dejected.

Ray came out and talked with her briefly. It seemed to be a friendly chat.

If she was skipping out on the rent, he didn't care. If she was being tossed out because she didn't have the rent, she didn't put up much of a fight. My guess was that she was leaving of her own accord. It would be hard for a social worker to afford an apartment by herself in Chinatown—or anywhere in the city, for that matter. And it was coming up to the first of the month.

A big yellow taxi found its way through the buildings like a big ship in a narrow harbor. The driver complained but helped her load her belongings. Should I follow? I couldn't, actually. Would she vanish?

Didn't matter. I couldn't do anything about it.

I moved down the street and sat on a step, waiting—for what, I wasn't sure. The question was, would I recognize it when it came? At one point, after an hour or so of waiting, I saw Mrs. Zheng and the little boy emerge. I couldn't imagine what I would learn from following them. But sometimes it's the seemingly ordinary act that reveals something important. She walked him to the park. And he wandered about from ladder to swing and from swing to slide.

Mrs. Zheng talked with another elderly Chinese lady. There were no smiles and no pauses in the conversation. There was nodding and frequent glances at the children. Afraid I'd be suspected of being a loitering pedophile, I went back to the Blue Dragon.

I wondered if Ted's things were still in the apartment. I would have loved to take a look through his belongings. However, I didn't want Ray to know I was outside the building, watching, staking it out, so I decided I'd wait until evening to check out Ted's apartment, now that his girlfriend was gone. I would come back dressed in my usual natty manner.

I must have missed those who went off to work early—Mr. Zheng, the Wens.

At nearly eleven, as the sun climbed down the brick walls of the buildings, Mr. Emmerich came out. He had a canvas bag in his hand and headed toward Stockton Street and its produce markets. I followed him.

He went to one of the larger markets. I watched as he haggled in Chinese with the woman behind the counter over the price of the oranges and later a twisted ginger-root. He was not a pleasant man. Voices were raised. A few people turned to look, but most didn't, and those who did turned away quickly. I assumed they knew him.

He made two more stops. He went inside a shop that appeared to specialize in herbs and teas. He picked up a Chinese newspaper. Then he headed back to the apartment.

If someone had come or gone in the interim, I had missed it. I waited and waited. At noon the narrow and comparatively quiet street was fully lit. Traffic had increased, and the plastic clicking of mahjong had begun.

A homeless man sat down beside me.

"You want to know how the universe began?" he asked.

"How?" I asked.

"A speck of sand." He was very brown, but beneath the dirt and tan, he was Caucasian. He had a dusty look—his face, his beard, his jacket, his pants and shoes. He looked like a large speck of sand himself.

"That's quite possible," I said.

Norman Chinn passed by. He had his briefcase and was heading toward the building. He looked bedraggled.

My new philosophical friend continued. "It was a perfect place, perfectly balanced in such a way that it didn't exist. And there came a speck of sand. And it disrupted the harmony of nothing and this"—he waved his hands broadly to encompass all of the world they could—"is the result."

I nodded.

"Do you believe that?" he asked.

"I believe that's possible," I said. "It's called the vacuum theory."

"What?"

"The world exists in a pristine state. Everything is symmetrical. And the introduction of a single particle—your grain of sand, for example—causes reality to come tumbling out."

"True?" he exclaimed in disbelief.

"I don't know. It's a theory."

"I'll be damned," he said. He stood up, shook his head and walked away, saying, "Crazy, crazy, crazy."

Mrs. Zheng came back with the little boy and a large bag of what I presumed to be food. She stopped in front of the door to get her keys. She dropped them. When she stooped down, she kissed the boy on the cheek, dabbed her thumb on her tongue and wiped away something above the boy's eye. She smiled. The boy smiled back. He reached out his arms, pulled her down so low she almost fell, and hugged her.

I stopped in at a small noodle joint. How out of touch I felt. When I'd finished eating I walked back out into the Chinatown street and its constant river of people, feeling that sense of not belonging more intensely than ever.

Norman Chinn was coming toward me. I brought the brim of my hat and my head down. I was sure he didn't notice me. A quick glance indicated that he had freshened up. He'd changed shirts and walked more briskly than before.

About four, as I began thinking about giving up, Steven Broder came out of the building. He was wearing a white shirt, black pants and shiny black shoes. Again, he carried a black jacket over his arm. I followed, but it was a long walk to a building that housed a catering firm. Others dressed like Steven entered or lounged around the doorway, smoking cigarettes.

Before he went inside, Steven turned in such a way that I could see him more clearly. The harsh light of the sun revealed a face more ravaged by time than I had realized when I'd seen him earlier in the hallway at the apartment building. He was even younger in the framed photograph in his and his lover's apartment.

Should I go back to the Blue Dragon or go home? Who else should I watch out for? The Wens would come home from work sometime after six. I decided to go see Ray in the evening and ask to go through—as ghoulish as it sounded to me—Ted Zheng's possessions or what was left of them.

Ray was there. When wasn't he? Initially, he pondered my request with consternation. But his obsession with participating in the investigation eventually won out in his quandary about the ethics of showing me Ted's things.

"I promised to box this stuff up for his parents," he said, still wary.

"Then I'll help," I said.

He smiled. Nodded. "Nothing wrong with that."

We went inside. Apartment 1B was in shambles. What else could anyone expect? Sandy Ferris had just extracted her life. That's what it looked like. There were empty spaces now, the physical manifestation of the emotion of leaving.

"Did Sandy Ferris leave you with an address?" I asked him.

"Oh yes. Forward mail. Phone number."

She wasn't running—or if she was, she certainly wasn't running smart.

"Why did she leave?"

"Couldn't pay rent alone. Have friend to stay with."

Ray went to find boxes. I went to the small battered desk and rummaged through the drawers. The first thing I found of interest was a bunch of old ledger sheets. These words were scrawled at the top: *Debt, parents*.

Underneath were dozens of entries, dating back several years. Simple addition and subtraction. It didn't take a professional accountant to make sense of them. Ted Zheng was more than fifty thousand dollars in debt to his parents. There were entries showing payments to them. But there were more frequent entries of larger amounts that only added to an ever-increasing debt.

I put these pages aside for later, more serious evaluation. I looked for letters. None. No diaries. I found a jewelry box. It had a velvet interior with specific places for cuff links and tie clasps and a space for other jewelry or mementos. The box was old and of European tradition, not Asian.

Inside the box were a couple of cuff links that didn't match, from a era that probably predated Ted Zheng. A plastic tortoiseshell ring, some rhinestones and two pins, one the shape of California. I found two keys as well. One still had its shine. The number 314 was etched in the shiny metal. It didn't look like a key to a serious lock. The other could have been a key to just about anything. Perhaps it was a spare to his apartment or to the front door. Or to another apartment.

At any rate, I wasn't sure I had found anything of value. Yet, since these items were in a lower drawer and in the back of that drawer, it seemed they were intentionally hidden.

I looked at the box more carefully. Not enough room for a hidden compartment. But I did notice that the velvet on the top was loose. I peeled away the corner and found a white envelope.

Inside was a photograph of Ted Zheng. I didn't know how recent it was. It seemed fairly recent, judging by the photo of him and Sandy I'd seen earlier. The only difference was that in this one Ted Zheng was as naked as can be, smiling big for the camera.

This perplexed me. The background of the photo was pretty nondescript. No telling where it had been taken. No telling why. But I was getting nervous. I was worried Ray might come in at any moment, so I put the photo back in the envelope and stuffed it and the ledger sheets into my jacket pocket. Then I remembered the keys. Might as well take them too. I had no idea what they unlocked, but if I came upon locks without keys, these might be what I'd need. I put the keys in my pocket.

When Ray came in, I was searching through Ted's clothing.

"Find anything?" Ray asked.

"People keep the strangest things, don't they?" I asked, to avoid having to lie.

I stayed an hour longer than I needed to, to help Ray feel his compromise was legitimate.

Once at home, I dumped out the contents of my search on the table in the dining room.

I took the photograph from the envelope. Yellow paint on the back of it. The room in which Ted Zheng was photographed looked a little more familiar now. The molding on the side of a door. Judging by the background, the photo had been taken in the empty apartment, the one Ted Zheng had been painting. But he was painting the apartment white, not yellow.

NINE

"You sure you don't want to rent 3B?" Ray said to me, grinning. "You here a lot, Mr. Chan." He'd interrupted a conversation he was having with Mrs. Zheng. I smiled in the direction of Mrs. Zheng, despite my irritation with Ray's needling references to the fictional detective Charlie Chan.

The little boy, hanging on to his grandmother's hand, twisted around to look at me. Eyes widened. He said something in Chinese. He kept his eyes fixed on me, obviously waiting for a reply.

"Hello," I said, knowing I had failed in some way.

The child's eyes went blank. Then he turned away.

Mrs. Zheng and Ray wound up their conversation. As the woman and her grand-child went past me to the door, the boy looked away sharply.

"Glad you are up and about," I said to Ray, who was smiling.

"Up early," he said. "Early bird catches the worm."

"Doesn't pay the worm to get up early then, does it?" I asked.

He looked at me like I was a fool. "You have solved the mystery?"

"No, but listen, uh...I found these keys and wondered who they might belong to."

"Where'd you find them?" Ray asked suspiciously. Ray was no fool. It was a fact I kept losing when he lapsed into his goofiness.

"On the stairway the other day. I just remembered."

"Let's see," he said with a knowing smile. "No one report a key missing." He handed back the smaller of the two keys. "I don't know about this one. Maybe small box. Maybe bicycle lock. I don't know."

"Not your mailboxes?"

"No, mailbox key even smaller. I don't know," he said.

I followed him into his apartment. He stopped just inside at a wooden board with eight hooks and keys.

"Mmmn," he said, examining the larger key. He began comparing its teeth with those of the keys on hooks. I was guessing it was a key to Ted's parents' apartment. Or, knowing that Ted had run some errands for Mrs. Ho and was painting apartments, it might be the key for 3B. But why had Ted hidden it?

"3A," Ray said. "Look."

"3A?"

He handed me the two keys. The teeth matched perfectly.

This was not what I wanted to hear. I had pretty much ruled out the Wens as irrelevant.

"You want key back?" He held it out to me as if he were the snake and this was the apple.

I took it and went upstairs to the empty apartment. I dismissed Ray's offer to accompany me. I compared the molding and floor with the photograph of naked Ted Zheng. There was a washed-out streak of white on the hardwood floor that told me exactly where the picture had been taken.

Next, I compared the yellow paint smudge on the back of the photo with the smudge on the canvas drop cloth. Another match. Ted or someone else had had fresh paint on his or her hands when they handled the photograph. And, if I wasn't mistaken, the color was the special one Ted had used in Norman and Steven's place.

I decided to wait. If Norman Chinn followed his routine, he would be home around lunchtime to freshen up and would leave again around two.

There would be a bit of a problem with this though. The yellow paint only indicated that Ted had handled the photograph at the same time he was using the yellow paint. The same paint as in the apartment occupied by Norman and Steven. It did not necessarily mean that either of the apartment occupants had anything to do with it. It did not mean that, but the implication was pretty clear nonetheless.

The problem was that even asking the question could be unnecessarily destructive. It could suggest or fuel a suspicion that might prove to be untrue. This could further tax what appeared to be an already fractious relationship.

And which of them should I approach first?

Either of them could have done this. It was clear that Steven found Asians attractive (at least one Asian anyway) or he wouldn't have settled in with Norman. It was clear that Norman liked younger men but was attracted to Asians as well.

I decided, rightly or wrongly, that Norman was the one I'd approach first, because he was the more mature. Steven, during our brief interaction, had seemed less patient and more likely to fly off the handle. With his apparent fondness for half-nude boys, Norman would have no grounds for righteous indignation.

I thought about all of this in the empty apartment. I was trying to imagine what set of circumstances would lead Norman or Steven to murder. Jealousy, of course. Blackmail. An unwelcome advance that led to a struggle that got out of hand.

The lobby beckoned. I didn't exactly want the company of Ray. On the other hand, I didn't want to miss Norman Chinn.

"Ted was a bit of a flirt?" I suggested to Ray as we stood in the small entry.

"Flirt?" Then he laughed and shook his head, no doubt at the images that appeared in his mind. "He take his shirt off, you know, walk around like a lion or something." Ray walked, moving his shoulders comically. "Not like Chinese to do that. His mother see him. She tell him to put on shirt and stop acting like that. She was ashamed of him. He laugh at her. Say this isn't China."

"And his father?" I asked.

"Nice man. Gentleman. I never see him tell his son bad things, you know." Ray seemed serious. "Mr. Zheng...Cheng Ye very nice man. If he want to say something to Ted, he take him into other room or something. Never in front of other people."

When Norman Chinn entered, he didn't look at us.

"Mr. Chinn," I said. He looked, nodded, went to the stairway. "I'm really sorry to disturb you, but I need a few more words with you, if you don't mind."

He stopped and turned toward me. He looked tired—exhausted, really. He looked at Ray, then back at me.

"Sure," he said. "I'll fix some coffee or something."

"Rough morning?" I asked as we went up the stairs. It was probably a rough night.

"When you get old, you forget more easily," Norman said. "Unfortunately, that means you forget you're getting old and do foolish things."

Inside his apartment, I declined a repeat of the offer for coffee, saying I wouldn't be that long. I knew he had things to do. A nap, probably.

"I'm afraid I'm going to have to be a little indiscreet," I told him.

He looked at me. His face was stone. Gave away nothing. I reached in my pocket and pulled out the photograph of Ted Zheng.

There wasn't one iota of surprise in his face. He knew the photograph.

"What of it?" he asked. The tone was conversational, not defensive.

"Did you take it?"

He was quiet. I took the picture to the wall, turned it over and let the yellow on the back of the photo touch the wall. Perfect match. I looked at him. He looked at me.

"Sit down, Mr. Strand."

"Peter."

"Peter."

He looked down at his feet, then up at me.

"I fall in love every day of my life. Some days I fall in love many times. I crave beauty. I'm addicted to it. It's harmless for the most part. Sometimes the objects of my desire are paintings, or flowers, or music, or furniture…whatever.

"For the most part, I am fickle about it," he continued. "The next day I see another painting or another chair. And I have a new love. The fickleness is a good thing. I am not wealthy enough, smart enough, young enough or good-looking enough to actually possess these objects. But that doesn't stop me from having these deep but fleeting infatuations."

Norman took a deep breath and continued. "All that being said, I am most deeply and totally and eternally in love with Steven. Though I hate him sometimes"—he laughed—"I cannot imagine life without him. Believe it or not, I rarely contemplate it. It is too frightening."

He paused again. It was as if he translated his thoughts in sections.

"Most Asians my age who grew up in the United States as I did received their cultural bearings not only from their families but from the popular culture. The Caucasian culture. The American culture. In those days the standards were completely and totally American. Cigarettes, movies, automobiles, fashion and celebrity.

"There was James Dean. And Marilyn Monroe. Elvis Presley and Cary Grant. There were no Asians. There were no Asian models in *Vogue* or *Esquire*. No Asians in *Playboy* magazine. No Asians in *The Young Physique* and *Demi-Gods*, where beautiful young white men wore nothing but a posing strap."

He looked at me, this time waiting for me to say something.

"I would think that you might understand what I'm saying," he said to my silence.

"I am following you," I said, giving nothing but what I had to give so he would continue.

"You'd think that at my age whatever was set in my psyche would be, in fact, set. That my libido was by now hardwired. Not totally, it appears. Ted triggered something. I felt giddy around him. Like a schoolboy recognizing beauty, sexual attraction, whatever, in my own race for the first time. And it was the first time I thought it was possible to find beauty in someone like me. In a Chinese boy."

"You hired him to paint your apartment," I said, not wanting to engage in this kind of conversation.

It was as if I had struck him. He sat back, disappointed. When he spoke again, it was dispassionately.

"As luck would or would not have it, yes. I told Ray I was looking for someone who could paint our apartment and he recommended Ted."

Again there was a moment of silence.

"I should have resisted, I suppose. For domestic bliss. It was warm, and he was an eager exhibitionist. He worked without his shirt. It didn't take long for such a foolish old man to do something stupid. Ted played me, but I wanted to be played, make no mistake about that."

"There is more," I said.

"Well...we didn't do anything. I mean, he and I didn't...ever. But there was conversation and teasing, and he agreed, for a small fee, to pose for me."

"You photographed in 3B? The empty apartment?"

"Yes."

"But there is yellow paint on the photograph."

"He wanted one photo, and I promised. I didn't get them back until after he was done with this room. But then I needed him to come back here. After Steven and

I got all the furniture in position and the paintings rehung, there were some places that needed to be touched up. That's when I gave him the photograph you have."

I waited.

He waited.

"So which of you killed him?" I asked.

"No, Mr. Strand. Neither of us. Your leap in logic is Olympian. It is not in my soul to destroy beauty."

"Blackmail."

"Me? We live in San Francisco, Mr. Strand, not Little Rock. No one cares about my sex life here."

"The police might suggest that you made unwanted advances and he reacted. There was a fight and—"

"Never."

"Steven."

"No."

"He knew about the photographs?"

"Yes."

"Maybe he and Ted argued."

"Steven was in Florida when Ted died."

"Why was he in Florida?"

"Looking for work." Norman looked at me and knew a question would come. He decided to answer it. "Despite my protestations, Steven didn't like my sudden appreciation of Asian beauty."

"I'm sorry. How does it stand?"

"Feebly here, it seems. With me, I mean. I'm not sure what's going through Steven's head. We aren't talking to each other about anything more serious than laundry detergent."

Norman Chinn looked drawn. If he was so concerned about the relationship, though, why was he out on the prowl last night? I didn't ask. As I started toward the door, he got up and came toward me.

"Could I have the photograph?" When I turned, he smiled. "Unless you like to look at naked Asian men."

"I can do that every time I shower. For now, that seems to be more than enough. I'll get this back to you when things are settled."

"You truly think someone in this building could have done it?"

"Yes."

"And are we high up on your list of suspects?"

"A little early for a rating."

As I exited, I ran into Steven on the stairway.

"Visiting Norman again?" he asked, eyebrow raised in an arched stereotype, voice carrying the dramatic innuendo.

"Just trying to figure out who did what to whom," I said.

"That's what I've been trying to do."

"I understand you were out of town at the time of Ted's death."

"I can supply you with a list of witnesses. Fortunately, I hate being alone. Apparently so does Norman."

"Very fortunate for you—I mean, to have witnesses."

"Blessed are the socially desperate," he said.

"Norman wasn't out of town, though, was he?"

"Norman just couldn't have, really. I'd like to hang him from the ceiling with tit clamps for his little obsessions. An old queer's dying search for perfect beauty, but that's what it's all about, isn't it?"

I went for a walk, eventually, to the charming streets near Jackson Square and then back to Mr. Zheng's Chinatown store. He seemed happy to see me.

"I'm sorry to keep barging in on you and bringing up painful subjects."

He put his hand on my shoulder. "No, no, you are a light in the darkness. I am glad to talk to you."

"I have a few questions," I said.

"Let's go grab a beer and talk."

He said something in Chinese to the young girl in the store. She smiled and waved.

"It is a double tragedy," Mr. Zheng said. "It is a tragedy for his mother and me. It is out of order. A break in the cycle. Children are not supposed to die before their parents. And then you think of it with the child in mind. Parents are supposed to be around to teach them about the world. It is the way. Yet it isn't."

I had nothing to say.

"But every human experiences tragedy, isn't that right, Peter?"

I nodded.

"We must get through it," he said, his hand on my shoulder. We walked to the same restaurant as before. We didn't bother with the separate little room, instead taking seats at the empty bar. The bartender and Mr. Zheng talked in Chinese. We were brought Budweisers.

"Ted owed you quite a bit of money," I said after we'd downed two good sips of beer each.

He shook his head.

"A son does not owe money to his father. It's all family. All the same thing. He was...irresponsible. It was difficult at times financially. His mother was so concerned about our old age. About the grandchild. My wife worries so much about such things. She is very pragmatic. She is very good with the inventory, very good with the accounts. I miss her at the shop. Except that she drove off other workers and some customers."

Mr. Zheng smiled and continued.

"Ted was a very happy boy. I wish he had inherited some of her common sense, her concentration. I wish she could have shared a little of his joy and his childish awe at the world and what it had to offer. Poor Gong Li. She has never left China."

"Don't you or your wife wonder who killed your son?"

"My wife knows. *America*. That was her last word on it."

He took a sip of beer, then angled his body toward me. "Now you, Peter Strand. Just who are you?"

TEN

I left Cheng Ye Zheng at the restaurant just past six. It was a short walk back to the Blue Dragon. I went around the block once to shake off the effects of the conversation. It had taken a few personal turns that I had hoped to avoid, but Mr. Zheng was convincing and forceful in his gentle way. I felt as if I'd said too much to him.

I was steady emotionally by the time I reached the apartment building and thought I was ready for May Wen. I *was* ready until she opened the door wearing a black slip and looking like a comic-book villainess—

a very sexy comic-book villainess. I went weak again quickly.

May gave me a face full of sensuous, dramatic boredom.

"A few more words, if you don't mind," I said without the nonchalance I had intended.

She stepped out of the way and shut the door behind me.

"No, leave it open," I said.

She shrugged and put the door ajar.

I took one of the keys, the larger one, out of my pocket and slipped it into the first of the two locks. The thick brassy deadbolt emerged from the door like an eager lover.

She looked at me silently.

I held the key up for her to see.

"So?"

"Came from Ted Zheng's secret box."

"A little pervert, huh?" She was unfazed.

I shut the door. "I don't know. Was he?"

"Maybe just a thief," she said, a teasing smile dancing on her face.

"Anything missing?"

"You tell me. You're the one nosing around," she said. She went into the room, picked up her cigarette case from the coffee table, pulled one out and lit it. Waited.

"Who was he visiting? You or your husband?"

"Why would he visit David?"

"Why would he visit you?"

"Are you slow on the uptake or trying to put me in my place?"

"You pick." I was getting stronger.

"Look, you are nobody I have to talk to," she said. "And I just got off work, and I don't feel like answering all your questions. All right?"

"Fine. Maybe your husband will answer them."

"He's out of town."

"I can find him."

Her eyes lowered briefly. "You a critic?"

"What was it? Drugs or sex? Or both?" I asked.

"People make much too big a deal out of both of them."

"How about murder? Are we making too much of it?"

She did her best to give me an ironic grin. "We had a little thing. It was completely harmless."

"Your husband know?"

"He knew I got some party favors from Ted."

"Party favors?"

She gave me the look. "How could you be so stupid?"

"Drugs."

"You make it sound so serious. A little something to enhance the music."

"And you and Ted…"

"Yes. A little tit for tat. How detailed do you want me to get?"

"Tell me just what you told your husband about it."

"You are a pain, Mr. Strand. He didn't know. He doesn't know. He doesn't have to know. You are going down the wrong street altogether. Nobody around here would kill Teddy. Even if my husband knew, he'd be mad at me, not Teddy. I've done it before, Mr. Strand. David takes the guy's side. Then he pouts for a day or two. Then we make passionate love and he starts thinking about his clients and...and...well..." She shrugged. "Listen, Teddy played around with drug dealers. Maybe he played a little harder than you think."

"Maybe."

"And me? Why would I do it? He was my source, and I enjoyed making payment."

When I returned home, I did something rare. I poured myself a gin and tonic.

May Wen's sexiness and nastiness had me twisted around. I paced awhile before remembering I still had the photograph of a naked man in my pocket. I took it out, and as I slid it back into the envelope for safekeeping, I discovered the check. It was nestled inside, against the back of the envelope. I'd missed it earlier.

The check was from the account of *Mrs. Kein Ho and Miss Barbara Siu.*

The address specified 3B, the vacant apartment. Mrs. Ho's.

It was a canceled check, number 1221, made out to FastMail. The check had been signed by Barbara Siu.

I found the number for Barbara and her sister. I went to the phone and dialed immediately, pacing and growing more impatient with each unanswered ring.

How could I have missed it? I thought. I was angry with myself, and I passed on a bit of that negative energy to Linda Siu when she answered.

"I'd like to speak with your sister," I said when she identified herself.

"That might be difficult. She's not here," said Linda, not intimidated by my unintentional cold tone.

"I'm sorry. I need to talk with her."

"There's something going on at the temple. I expect her back before ten. Is there something I can help you with?"

I considered telling her. I decided not to. I didn't want to give the two of them time to cook something up if something needed cooking.

"You mind if I come over then?"

There was a long pause. Finally a hesitant no. Then she added, "Are you sure you can't tell me what this is about?"

"I'd rather address it with the two of you," I said, but I wasn't altogether sure that was true. I'd just as soon not have Linda around when I brought up the subject.

Barbara Siu was exceptionally flighty. Linda Siu seemed to counter by being exceptionally tough and abrasive.

I politely refused the offer of tea, claiming it was too late. However, my reticence came from the manner in which Mrs. Ho might have met her death. Daily tea containing doses of any one of a number of poisons could drive a woman crazy. Crazy enough to venture into an empty elevator shaft. Crazy enough to be easily guided to an empty elevator shaft. Such a frail body could easily have thrown off its mortal coil with the help of the tiniest of shoves.

"What is it that you want of us?" Linda asked.

"I want to find out a little more about your relationship with Mrs. Ho."

"Mrs. Ho?" Linda said, surprised, then indignant. "I thought you were investigating the death of the young man."

Barbara seemed to cower from the increased volume of her sister's thought.

Demurely, Barbara stepped closer and spoke in halting English. "In afternoon I take tea to her."

"My sister cared for Mrs. Ho," Linda said. "Helped her. Did her shopping. Cleaned her apartment. Gave her baths when it became necessary. Why are you questioning us?"

"Just trying to find out about Mrs. Ho and Ted Zheng."

"You've talked to us once. We told you what we knew. That should be enough," Linda said.

"I'm really sorry. But I wasn't aware of the death of Mrs. Ho at the time."

"Mrs. Ho's death was an accident. What are you trying to do, Mr. Strand? Mr. Lehr pays you by the hour and you have to dredge up something more to keep busy?"

Linda wasn't just impatient—she was angry.

"I found this check." I showed it to both of them.

"So?"

"I found it in Ted's belongings."

"I don't know why he had it, but I certainly don't know what it has to do with anything."

"He had it in a secret place where it would be away from prying eyes."

"I don't understand..."

Barbara said something in Chinese, then turned to me. "Mrs. Ho and I went to bank. She set up account so I can buy things for her."

With that Barbara left the room, leaving me with a seething Linda Siu.

"Barbara is the most wonderful person in the world. She is also very easily upset. So help me, Mr. Strand, if..."

Barbara returned carrying a cardboard shoe box.

"You see," Barbara said. "Everything in here." She lifted the lid. There were checks in short stacks secured with rubber bands. There were two dozen or so envelopes containing what looked like bank statements. There was the checkbook. "You look carefully. I do not cheat Mrs. Ho."

I felt ashamed, though I had done nothing other than ask what I thought were reasonable questions.

But Barbara's eyes were pleading for me to believe her.

"May I take these with me?" I asked Barbara.

Barbara nodded.

I left feeling troubled. It is always troubling to see a relationship when one person seems so dominant, so forceful, and the other so submissive, so weak. Was Linda a wonderful older sister protecting an innocent and shy person from the evils of the world? Or had she created it, denying the full expression of life from someone who could be dominated?

I turned back as I was leaving to see the tough sister comforting the other. If it was love...

ELEVEN

A bottle of Caymus Conundrum, uncorked. Music, soft but unobtrusive. Music to do accounting by. I had the checking-account statements and returned checks in front of me. Drinking and accounting might not normally be compatible activities, but this was far from high finance.

Some of the payees were impossible to make out. But by and large the names were evident in the endorsements—grocers, pharmacies and the like. The only major expense was the rent, which was paid on the last day of the month.

There was never enough money in the account to do any real damage—rarely much more than enough to cover the month's expenses. Periodically there was a deposit. A standard amount at a regular frequency. Obviously, money came from somewhere else. A savings account, an investment portfolio or a trust. Whatever. But as far as I knew, these other funds were not accessible by Barbara Siu.

It didn't take long. When the account was balanced, there was still half a bottle of wine left.

I went to the garden and looked out into the twinkling night. Something was changing. This whole thing, this investigation, had been more than what it appeared. I wasn't just investigating other people. What I'd told Cheng Ye Zheng that afternoon in the bar...these were things I'd never told anyone. I'd told him about being four years old and standing outside the wrecked car and seeing my parents. Remembering them not as humans but simply as masks. As pretend.

At first he'd said nothing. He just put his arm around me. Finally he said, "They were dead. The spirits were gone. They really were masks. But you will know them again one day. They are you, you know."

He took his hand away, took another sip of his beer. "Poor Gong Li," he said. "She sees Ted in the boy. She is determined to get it right this time. It is not so easy, I tell her. Love is not like a business." He laughed.

He took a last sip, threw some bills on the counter and pulled me off the high seat. "Ah," he said, "it all depends on how you look at things. Sometimes you are looking at the right thing but in the wrong place."

I'd walked him back to his shop then, seeing all those faces, all those people, more directly connected to their pasts. Ancestors. Families.

I shook off the memories of the afternoon, leaving Mr. Zheng back in Chinatown. I walked through my dining room, clearing dishes. But I was drawn back to the check I'd retrieved from Ted Zheng's secret spot.

I knew. I suppose it had been brewing just beneath my consciousness. The answer seemed certain. It was all so simple. And if I was right, it was all so…provable.

Morning came gray and threatening. Clouds swept in. I could see them coming, angry swirls sweeping through the gaps in the hills. I could feel the moisture on my cheeks as I descended the Saturn Street Steps. In moments I couldn't see beyond the railing, and it seemed as if I were floating in a cold, barren limbo. At the bottom, a short, damp walk through a quiet residential neighborhood brought me to Castro and Market, a transportation hub minutes from the heart of the city.

The Municipal Railway cars were crowded, and everything smelled of wet wool and influenza. Off the train at Powell station. All was quiet there. Perhaps for the first time, there was no tourist line for the cable cars. All the musicians had departed, and those who preached damnation had had their hellfires drenched.

Only a few straggling souls scurried across the open area, umbrellas suddenly swept up like cups on stems.

It could have waited, I told myself. I searched Market Street for taxis. Never in the rain. Never, never in the rain.

I walked and walked until finally I was at the soft, undefined edge of the financial district. Here the cold, clean buildings buzzed with electronic debits and credits. Here too was the beginning of North Beach and Little Italy. All the great food and coffee and pastry and a sleazy sprinkling of X-rated video arcades and lap dancers.

Here was FastMail the branch closest to Chinatown. It was a hole in the wall that had a counter at one end. The room was lined on one side with packing and mailing materials and on the other with rows and rows of keyed boxes with numbers on them. Personal mailboxes.

The key in my pocket said 314. I followed the logical path to a medium-sized mailbox. There were letters inside addressed to Mrs. Ho—a newsletter from a hospital, envelopes from Pacific Gas and Electric and from Pacific Telephone. There was a post-card from a jeweler announcing a sale. The box was full. Advertisements mostly.

More important, there was a large manila envelope containing several sheets of legal-sized paper.

A will. Mrs. Ho's will.

I'd found what I was looking for. Maybe more. Instead of using a lockbox in a bank, Mrs. Ho had used her mailbox as a place to keep a copy of her will. Or someone had.

My hands were cold as I unfolded the papers. There were two sets. One in English. One in Chinese. I moved quickly through the English version, skipping the words common to all wills.

There was the name—the lone benefactor.

Out in the cold rain and back in Chinatown, I walked up the street that ran by the sad, empty playground. The wind whipped the swings, the chains making a hollow sound as they clanged against the metal swing set. The rain was horizontal.

The apartment building looked more ragged and old in the dismal light. I buzzed.

Ray came to the door, smiling. "You are very brave detective," he said. "You come out on a day like this. Very brave."

I climbed the steps. The door to 4B was ajar as usual. I called out his name. Wallace Emmerich didn't answer. I edged inside.

I looked around. He wasn't there.

I had started back down the stairs when I remembered the narrow stairway to the roof. At the top, the door to the roof was propped open. The rain was still strong, and now the wind was slashing out as well.

Wallace Emmerich, in his long dark-blue robe, was trying to throw a sheet of plastic over some of his plants. It was sheer madness. As soon as he got one corner secure, he'd move to another only to have the first rip free again.

"Mr. Emmerich!" I called out. The wind blew his name back against my own ears.

He couldn't hear me.

I helped Emmerich secure the plastic over the plants. He didn't question the act at all. We worked together until finally it was done.

Then Emmerich looked at me. He knew then. He knew then that I knew.

His look was one of pure anger.

"So!" he yelled. "You'll never prove it."

I went to him. The rain now drenched us both.

"Oh yes I will. I *have*," I said, guiding his body to the door and down the steps. "I found the will," I said when we'd finally maneuvered our soaked bodies into his apartment. Inside, the sound of rain crashing against the windows was muffled some, but we could still hear the wind as the storm continued to rage.

"The will?" Emmerich said. He looked confused.

"Mrs. Ho's."

His face went blank. His *never prove it* was aimed at the murder of Ted Zheng.

"A little foxglove. Digitalis. In small doses with her evening tea. Not enough to kill her. Enough to drive her mad, however. Enough to fool her into signing a will. What did she think she was signing? A lease maybe? A petition? Could have been anything."

Emmerich was quiet. His eyes looked like glass.

"And you killed Ted Zheng because he was either blackmailing you over her death or maybe because he found out and just didn't like it."

"Even if all that were so, Mr. Strand, you could not prove what you say."

"Mrs. Ho's body can be exhumed and tested. I guarantee you, they can find trace chemicals these days."

"Even if that were true, there is no way I can be singled out. I think you are venturing entirely beyond your capacity."

His narrow smile accompanied a bitter but triumphant stare.

"Mr. Emmerich?" I was about to steal victory from him.

He looked at me, his head high, eyes peering down, the cold smile still on his face.

"How did your wife die?" I asked.

Only his eyes gave him away. I went on.

"The key here, Mr. Emmerich, is the exhumation of your wife. I'd be willing to bet—and you aren't a betting man, are you, Mr. Emmerich?—that substantial traces of digitalis will be found in your wife's remains as well."

He was quiet. Very quiet.

"What we have, Mr. Emmerich, is all we need in a murder investigation. Means. Motive. Opportunity. Weapon. And bodies. Three of them."

The rain stopped. The wind stopped. It was strangely quiet.

Emmerich stood in the middle of his apartment, dripping water on the floor. I went into the bathroom and grabbed a towel.

I helped him change and dry off before I called the police.

"I don't want my wife's body exhumed. Oh, please don't."

"It's not up to me. But I doubt if they'll need to if you confess."

He looked around his apartment. He looked forlorn. Lost. Suddenly, he pulled himself together. He looked at me angrily.

"How was I supposed to live?" he asked.

Wallace Emmerich was docile when the police came. Foolishly, perhaps, and despite the reading of his rights, he made a complete statement. I stayed to listen because there was one important question left to answer.

Why, precisely, was Ted Zheng killed? Ted had put the pieces together as well. The discovery of the will. Ted had wanted to verify his suspicions with Wallace

Emmerich. Emmerich baited him to the basement to show him proof that the elevator death was an accident. That's where and when Emmerich had struck him with a lead pipe.

with their royal-blue flow...
a bed of flowers...

TWELVE

A month, perhaps more, passed before I realized I still had the key to apartment 3A. Maybe it was only an excuse to go to Chinatown. I'm not sure. Besides returning the key, I really had no other reason to go to that part of the city.

This time, my trip down the Saturn Street Steps was in the sunshine. Out in front of me was the blue sky. Absolutely clear. The jacaranda trees were in bloom with their royal-blue flowers. Below them, a bed of flowers also exploded with blue blossoms. What a wondrous day! I thought. It was summer now.

The narrow street where the Blue Dragon lived was lit by the noon sun too. And there was Ray Leu, standing outside saying goodbye to an elderly Chinese couple.

Ray shook his head in disbelief. He laughed.

"Mr. Chan. Mr. Private Detective. You did good job, eh?"

"I have that key," I said, fishing it out of my pocket. "For 3A."

Ray nodded. "The Wens. Gone now."

"Really."

He shook his head. "Much change. You know Mr. Emmerich is gone. Sandy Ferris is gone. Mr. Chinn's boyfriend...pfft. All white people gone." He laughed.

I didn't know whether the white people being gone was bad or good, but apparently it was notable.

"Wens move to Russian Hill somewhere."

"The sisters?"

"Here. So are Cheng Ye Zheng and his wife and the little boy."

"Good," I said. "So you have lots of apartments to rent?"

"Yes, you want one?"

For a moment I tried to imagine myself living in Chinatown.

"That would be an adventure," I said.

"Cheng Ye ask about you. You should go see him. He like you very much. He said you are 'fine boy.'"

Ray patted me on the back.

Once out in the narrow street, I turned back. Mrs. Zheng was with the child. She looked down at him, saying something I couldn't hear as they walked hand in hand.

I felt warm and sad.

ACKNOWLEDGMENTS

A special thanks to Guolin Tao. Thanks also to the usual suspects—brothers Richard and Ryan as well as Jovanne Reilly and David Anderson.

RONALD TIERNEY'S *The Stone Veil* introduced semi-retired private investigator "Deets" Shanahan. The book was nominated for the Private Eye Writers of America's Shamus Award for Best First Novel. The most recent, *Killing Frost,* is the eleventh in the series *Booklist* said was "packed with new angles and delights."

Before writing mysteries, Tierney was founding editor of *NUVO,* an Indianapolis alternative newspaper, and the editor of several other periodicals. The author lives in San Francisco, where he continues to write. For more information, visit www.ronaldtierney.com.

Scenes from **The Black Tortoise,**
book two in the Peter Strand series

I'm a little bit of a puzzle, I'm afraid. I look
Chinese. That's because I'm half Chinese and
half Cherokee. Unfortunately, I never knew my
parents, a story for later maybe. I was adopted
by an elderly white couple from Phoenix.
I speak English, no Chinese. But in keeping
with the stereotype, I'm very good at math.
I became an accountant, one who specializes in
forensic accounting, which means I investigate
criminals, people who try to cook the books.
I also acquired a private investigator's license
when I moved to San Francisco.

I've never met Mr. Lehr, though he is my
major client. I talk to him on the phone, or we
converse by email. He is an important man in the
city. He owns a lot of property, from which he
earns a handsome living. I help him by looking

into his investments for signs of fraud, embezzlement or kickbacks— any criminal behavior tied to the handling of money.

My private investigator's license allows me to look into the past behavior and associations of people with whom Mr. Lehr does or might do business.

"Strand, listen," Lehr said in a gravelly whisper. "You know the Fog City Arts Center? I'm on their board. Some crazy shit is going on down here. The staff is ready to mutiny. I told the board you'd go down, look into things."

"What things?"

"The crazy stuff. You need to see Madeline Creighton. She's the executive director. So arrange things and straighten it out."

A good walk clears the brain, I've found. As I was walking to the arts center the next morning, I mulled over the events of the evening before. I realized that aside from mad Madeline, Emelio had already introduced me at his party to the key players—the family-oriented sales guy Craig Anglim, the attractive events overseer Vanessa Medder and down-to-earth architect Marguerite Woodson—the people I most wanted to interview. These three—five, including Madeline and Emelio—were in the best position to have access to substantial amounts of money.

The doors to the foundation were locked. The hours of operation painted on the glass doors told me I was fifteen minutes early.

I heard the water lapping at the pilings. I went to the edge and looked over. To my surprise there was a large turtle, a sea turtle. Its dark, shiny shell might have been five feet long. When our eyes met, it disappeared.

What a strange creature. A living being with its own mobile home. The moment it is observed, it hides— in the ocean or in its shell. We can see it, but only as much as it wants us to see. As is the case with all of us, it cannot completely ignore reality, but, more than most of us, it can withdraw from it.